the new batch

Cupcake Diaries

Ren's One-of-a-Kind Cupcakes

By Coco Simon
author of Cupcake Diaries

Illustrated by Manuela López

Simon Spotlight
New York London Toronto Sydney New Delhi

This book is a work of fiction. Any references to historical events, real people, or real places are used fictitiously. Other names, characters, places, and events are products of the author's imagination, and any resemblance to actual events or places or persons, living or dead, is entirely coincidental.

SIMON SPOTLIGHT
An imprint of Simon & Schuster Children's Publishing Division
1230 Avenue of the Americas, New York, New York 10020
This Simon Spotlight edition August 2024
Copyright © 2024 by Simon & Schuster, LLC
All rights reserved, including the right of reproduction in whole or in part in any form.
SIMON SPOTLIGHT and colophon are registered trademarks of Simon & Schuster, LLC.
Simon & Schuster: Celebrating 100 Years of Publishing in 2024
For information about special discounts for bulk purchases, please contact
Simon & Schuster Special Sales at 1-866-506-1949 or business@simonandschuster.com.
Text by Mei Nakamura
Designed by Brittany Fetcho
Illustrations by Manuela López
The illustrations for this book were rendered digitally.
The text of this book was set in Bembo Std.
Manufactured in the United States of America 0724 LAK
2 4 6 8 10 9 7 5 3 1
ISBN 978-1-6659-5922-3 (pbk)
ISBN 978-1-6659-5923-0 (hc)
ISBN 978-1-6659-5924-7 (ebook)
Library of Congress Catalog Card Number 2024933388

CONTENTS

Chapter 1: Project Renway — 1

Chapter 2: Under Ren's Roof — 23

Chapter 3: Bitter Feelings — 31

Chapter 4: A Missing Piece — 47

Chapter 5: Cupcake Complications — 59

Chapter 6: A Complete Batch of Bakers — 69

Chapter 7: Special Delivery for a Special Friend — 81

Chapter 8: The Mini Cupcake Club of Kindness — 87

Chapter 1

Project Renway

"Did everyone get a chance to take their turn during today's popcorn reading?" Mrs. Nelson scanned the room while everyone nodded yes, except for me. I love playing popcorn—it's one of the few times I actually feel comfortable enough to speak aloud in class—but today I was skipped. *Why am I surprised?* I thought.

I just moved here, and being in a new

school filled with people who already know one another is really hard. And I can be kind of quiet until you get to know me, so it's a bit harder for me to make friends.

Rrriing!

The sound of the bell was music to my ears. It was lunchtime! I shut my history textbook and stuffed it in my backpack. As soon as I was in the hallway, I made a beeline for the cafeteria.

At the start of the Fenton Street School year, I felt pretty lonely. But then I met Alana, Natalie, and Emily, and things have been great since then! We formed the Mini Cupcake Club, and we even won a baking competition with our first-ever entry: mini chocolate cupcakes with a cinnamon twist, topped with a family recipe for salted caramel frosting from Natalie's *abuela*!

Right before I made the final turn toward the cafeteria's double doors, I heard my name.

"Hey, Ren! Wait up!" I stopped in my tracks. It wasn't a girl's voice, so who else would be calling my name in the hallway? I don't really know anyone other than the members of the Mini Cupcake Club.

That meant it could only be one person. I turned and saw him.

"Hi, Ethan!" Ethan helps out with the Mini Cupcake Club. Sometimes he gets wild ideas for cupcake flavors, but he's also a super hard worker and a lot of fun to be around.

As we headed to lunch together, we saw a colorful poster taped to the wall. KINDNESS WEEK was written on the top in big bold letters.

Ethan and I stopped to read it. We learned that next week, Fenton would be offering lots of activities to encourage us to be kinder to one another. Students were invited to write poetry and make artwork about kindness that would be displayed in the hallways. There were even music and dance events planned in the gym after classes.

As I read, I felt a flicker of excitement. "I wonder if we can make cupcakes for all our classmates during Kindness Week?" I said to Ethan. "After all, what's kinder than cupcakes?"

Ethan grinned. "I love it! Let's show the school how much we care, cupcake-style!"

"But first . . . lunch," I said.

Ethan laughed, and we raced to the cafeteria. By the time Ethan and I got to our usual table, Alana was already there. Alana is our club's manager, which means she keeps track of our baking events and makes sure we don't overbook our calendar.

"What's new, Ren?" she asked me.

"I've got an idea for Kindness Week!" I told Alana about making cupcakes for students.

"That's awesome!" Alana liked the idea so much, she bounced in her seat a little. "Maybe we could make a different flavor for every activity. With a different design for each one too! Ethan, you could totally come up with some rad flavors!"

I paused. I really like Alana, but this was *my* idea. I wanted to be in charge of it and take the lead for once. "Maybe," I said, and then turned to Ethan to change the subject. "Hey, you were amazing in the basketball game yesterday afternoon!"

Just then the other two members of the Mini Cupcake Club, Natalie and Emily, joined us at our table. They were deep in conversation about the new soccer cleats that Natalie wants. They said hi to us and immediately went back to their discussion.

For the rest of lunch, Ethan, Alana, and I talked about Ethan's winning basket. I thought I'd dodged Alana's ideas, but later that night she called me.

"What's up, Alana?"

"I've got it all planned out," she said.

I sighed. "I kind of would like . . ."

"Just hear me out," she continued. "For the library, we can make cupcakes with rainbow frosting and little letter sprinkles."

I frowned. "That could be fun, but—"

"And then for the music events, we could decorate the tops with little musical notes cut out of fruit leather! You're already an expert at that!" said Alana.

"Alana!" I knew I said her name a little too loudly, but I was tired of feeling ignored. "I don't need your help. I just wanted to know if you liked the idea."

"Oh," Alana said. There was a pause. "So . . . you don't want to hear what else I came up with?"

"No. Ethan and I will handle everything," I blurted out.

"Well, fine," Alana said in a weird voice.

"See you tomorrow at school," I said, and we hung up.

I sat with the tablet on my lap for a few seconds with a weird feeling I couldn't put my finger on. That was the shortest conversation I'd ever had with Alana. I started feeling guilty and thought about calling her back, but then I decided to call Ethan instead.

The more I thought about it, the more I didn't want to discuss my idea with Emily and Natalie, either. I wanted to show everyone that Ethan and I could do this on our own. I gave him a call.

"Hey, can you come over tomorrow after basketball practice so we can plan our Kindness Week cupcakes?" I asked him.

"I'll ask my parents, but I'm sure they'll say yes," Ethan said cheerfully.

"Great." I took a deep breath. "One more thing. Could you not tell Emily and Natalie about our idea?"

He didn't say anything for a while. "Okay, but why?" he asked.

"It's our idea, and we don't need anyone's help. We got this," I told him. "The Mini Cupcake Club has other projects right now, and I know they'll be really impressed and happy for us when we pull this off."

"Are you sure, Ren?" Ethan asked.

"I'm sure," I said firmly.

Chapter 2

Under Ren's Roof

The next day, Ethan and I met at my place to figure out our plan for Kindness Week. As Ethan walked into my house, he sniffed the air with a big smile on his face. "What smells so good?" he asked.

I told Ethan my dad was making homemade spring rolls. "My dad loves to cook, especially his mother's recipes. He usually doesn't let us have anything before dinner, but maybe because you're a guest, he'll make an exception." I turned toward the kitchen. "Hey, Dad!" I called.

Right on cue, my dad came out of the kitchen holding a tray with two spring rolls on it, a pitcher of ice water, and two glasses.

He grinned at Ethan and me. "Just one each. I don't want you to spoil your appetites," he said.

"Thank you, Mr. Lu," Ethan said.

Ethan and I both took big bites out of the rolls. *Mmm,* they were still warm and so crunchy! My dad said to let him know if we needed anything else, and he headed into the living room.

As the Mini Cupcake Club's official decorator, I thought I'd start with discussing the decorations first.

"What do you think about wrapping the cupcakes in clear cellophane tied with colorful ribbons?" I suggested. "It will make each cupcake feel individual and special."

"That's great!" Ethan's eyes lit up. "We can make one for every student in our grade. And we'll get to school early on the first day of Kindness Week and leave one on each desk as a surprise."

"I love it!" I said. "First, we'll need to clear it with Principal Estrella."

Ethan nodded. "We can give each member of the club a bunch to deliver so we don't miss anyone's desk—including the teachers'!"

"Umm . . . let's talk about who's doing what later," I said. I knew what Ethan meant—it would be faster and easier if the entire Mini Cupcake Club helped—but I still wanted just the two of us to take care of everything.

"Next we need to figure out what kind of cupcakes we want to make, as well as the kind of frosting we want on them," Ethan continued. "And then we actually have to *make* all the cupcakes . . . and then deliver them to every classroom in our grade." He stopped and looked at me. "That's a lot of work. Are you sure you don't want to involve the rest of the club?"

"We'll find a way to make it work by ourselves," I told Ethan. "I promise."

Chapter 3

Bitter feelings

The following afternoon, the Mini Cupcake Club met at my house, as we'd planned last week. We had two big orders to fill: one for the next Parent-Teacher Association meeting, and the other for Alana's grandmother's birthday.

When Alana arrived, she greeted me with a flat, "Hey."

"Hi," I said back, just as flatly.

Alana went inside without another

word. Alana was clearly still upset about our conversation. A few moments later, Ethan, Emily, and Natalie arrived, and we got to work.

We'd decided to make lemon cupcakes with orange-flavored frosting, topped with tiny black licorice twists that spelled out "PTA." As I started decorating the batch that was ready, Alana sniffed.

"You know, a lot of people don't like licorice. Just because it's easy to form into shapes doesn't mean it'll taste good," Alana told me.

I popped a piece of licorice in my mouth. The flavor was strong and weirdly bitter. But I didn't tell her that. Instead, I said, "Well, lots of other people love licorice. And you're not the official decorator of this club, anyway."

Emily frowned. "Is something going on with you two?"

"No," Alana and I said together.

After we were finished with the PTA cupcakes, my mom came into the kitchen.

"Who wants a snack?" she asked.

"I do!" I immediately answered.

"How about some sliced fruit?" my mom suggested. "Kids, why don't you all go in the living room and hang out while Ren and I prepare everything."

Everyone smiled and thanked my mom before heading into the living room.

"Please get some apples and oranges from the fridge," Mom said.

As I rummaged through the fridge, my mom spoke softly behind me. "It sounds like you and Alana are having some trouble."

I shrugged and brought her four apples and three oranges. "It's no big deal."

"Does this have anything to do with the cupcakes you're making with Ethan for Kindness Week?" she asked me.

Moms. They know everything, don't they?

"Maybe," I said.

"You know, you and Ethan have a lot of work cut out for you. Sometimes it's okay to get help from people who want to give it and not let pride get in the way." Mom finished cutting the fruit into slices and arranged them beautifully on a serving platter.

I sighed. "But Alana kept interrupting me on the phone, I couldn't even get a word in, and the kindness cupcakes were my idea."

My mom started to answer, but just then Ethan came into the kitchen. "This looks great!" he said, picking up the plate.

"Let me know when you're ready to bake your next batch of cupcakes," Mom said. "No touching the oven without me in the room."

I nodded and then followed Ethan into the living room. We all sat on the big sofa, munching but not having any conversations with one another. Finally, Emily turned to Alana and me.

"Before we start in on the cupcakes for Alana's grandma, are you two going to tell us what's going on?" she asked.

"Yeah, we're friends! We should be able to talk about anything," Natalie added.

I thought about what my mom had said. About letting friends help. Maybe she was right. But before I could say anything, Alana spoke up.

"It's between Ren and me," she said.

If Alana felt that way, then I did too. I nodded and brought the empty plate back into the kitchen.

We got to work on our next round of cupcakes, but no one talked much.

In fact, there was a kind of sad silence the whole time, with the occasional eyes darting back and forth between everyone awkwardly, until the orders were done. And then it was time for everyone to go home.

Chapter 4

A Missing Piece

The next day when I reached our lunch table, I found Ethan there but no Alana.

"She's sitting somewhere else today," Ethan told me.

At first, I felt pretty bad, but then I got a little annoyed. I couldn't believe she'd actually moved to another table.

"We've got to discuss flavors," I said, taking a notebook and pen out of my backpack. "What do you think about red velvet mini cupcakes with white icing and little candy hearts?"

"Is that too lovey?" Ethan asked.

"Okay, how about mini vanilla cupcakes with lemon icing?" I said.

"I don't know," Ethan replied. "That seems too . . . vanilla?"

I frowned. "Why are you having problems with all my suggestions?"

Ethan shook his head. "No, it's not that. If we're making cupcakes for everyone in our grade, I just think they should be more personalized or specific to Kindness Week. Maybe—"

I waved my hand for Ethan to stop talking. "Shh! Here come Natalie and Emily," I said. "We'll talk more later."

I had never shushed someone before. It felt different. And not a good kind of different. Doing the shushing, I realized, feels just as bad as being shushed.

Natalie and Emily sat down. They were both giggling, but they stopped when they noticed Alana wasn't there. To fill the silence, I announced, "Alana's sitting with another friend today. No big deal." Natalie and Emily exchanged a look but didn't say anything.

"Natalie was just telling me about an idea she has for springtime cupcakes," Emily said. "Little cupcakes that look like baby chicks!"

"They can be frosted yellow and sprinkled with coconut flakes to make them look fuzzy!" Natalie added, finishing her idea off with a cheerful giggle.

"So cute!" Emily said. "It makes me think about doing a whole assortment of mini cupcakes that look like other baby animals, like puppies and kittens."

"That's a fun idea," I agreed. "I know people like to throw parties for their pets' birthdays. We could offer mini cupcakes that look like their pets!"

"We could even make cupcakes for the dogs to eat!" Ethan added. "Of course, we'd have to use different ingredients and make sure they're safe for dogs."

We all sat around and talked and laughed about baby animal cupcakes for the rest of our lunch period. I couldn't help but think about Alana. *She would love this,* I thought. I could just imagine her making a list of holidays and special animal-themed mini cupcakes to go with them. I looked around the table and thought about how much fun it was when we were all together bouncing ideas off one another.

Then I remembered my mom's advice again, about accepting help from people who want to give it. The problem was, I didn't think my mom understood that this was my first creative cupcake idea. Being shy and quiet, I usually keep my ideas to myself. This time, I wanted to prove to everyone, including myself, that my great idea could be a success.

Still, I missed Alana. Here we all were, laughing and having a good time. Everyone seemed to forget that Alana wasn't there. Except for me.

Chapter 5

Cupcake Complications

That afternoon, after discussing numerous flavor combinations on our tablets, Ethan and I finally decided on layered rainbow cupcakes with a short and sweet message written on top. I couldn't wait to start making them!

We needed to make sixty-five cupcakes, for three classes with twenty students each, plus three for the teachers and two teacher's aides. On Sunday,

Ethan came over to my house to make them. As usual, my parents were around to supervise the baking.

The baking part was easy. We made a vanilla batter and divided it into five bowls. Then we added food coloring to each bowl to make our rainbow colors: violet, blue, green, yellow, and red. Next, we carefully spooned a layer of each color into the cupcake liners, trying our best to make them all even. We made a dozen extra cupcakes in case we messed up with a few of them.

After they were done baking and had cooled, I carefully peeled the liner off one cupcake.

It was perfect—a fantastic little rainbow! Our method worked! Then it was time to decorate, my specialty. I frosted a cupcake with chocolate frosting, then dumped out a bag of tiny candy letters and numbers that my mom and I had bought at the grocery store. I wanted to write little messages like U R GR8, B KIND, and B HAPPY. But I couldn't get

more than two candies on the frosting before the top of the cupcake was completely full.

"Huh. Maybe we just buy some heart candies, like the kind for Valentine's Day? The messages on them are pretty much the same as the ones we want to use."

Ethan said, "No! That would be cheating. If we go with heart candies, the decorations aren't going to be special."

"Okay, let's try piping the messages on the cupcakes instead," I suggested. I got out my mom's piping kit and found the thinnest tip. Then I loaded a small amount of vanilla frosting into the piping bag.

I managed to spell out U R GR8 on the test cupcake, but it took about ten minutes because I messed up three times in a row and had to start over.

"Let me try," Ethan said. He took the piping bag and tried to spell U R SWEET, but his letters were way too big and he only got to U R SW before he ran out of room.

I sighed. "This isn't working. We only have eight spare cupcakes left, and we've only made one good cupcake."

"Yeah." Ethan's face fell as he set down the piping bag.

Looking at him, I realized I'd let my friend down. I had been so stubborn about making the kindness cupcakes by ourselves, I'd ignored his idea to include the rest of the Mini Cupcake Club.

I couldn't let Ethan down even more. I couldn't let *myself* down. And I couldn't let my friends in the Mini Cupcake Club down. I knew what I had to do.

"Ethan, please hand me my tablet," I said. "It's time for me to set things right."

Chapter 6

A Complete Batch of Bakers

When I had my tablet, I messaged Alana, Natalie, and Emily. I told them to come over, but I didn't tell them for what. Alana replied that she was helping her mom watch her two little brothers, so could we all meet at her house instead? Luckily, everyone said yes.

So Ethan and I enthusiastically packed up our baking supplies and carefully arranged the baked cupcakes in plastic containers to show the rest of the group how far we'd gotten.

When we got to Alana's house, her little brothers were playing a loud game of tag in the living room. Alana picked up two toy trucks and asked the boys to play with their trucks while she talked with her friends. I stood in front of everyone seated on the couch and took a deep breath.

"I want to say I'm sorry," I started. I turned to Ethan. "I'm sorry I didn't listen to your advice about including the rest of the club. I told you I wanted this to be our project, and instead, I acted like a mean boss."

Then I turned to Alana. "I especially want to say I'm sorry to you. When I came up with the idea of kindness cupcakes for the event at school, it was the first cupcake project I'd thought of by myself. But when you had all those plans, I thought the idea wouldn't belong to me anymore. Leading comes so easy for you, and I really wanted to show everyone—including myself—that I could be a leader too."

Alana's eyes grew wide. "I was just excited to help. You are a leader, Ren. We all take turns leading this club together. It's impossible for just one person to do everything on their own." Alana stood to give me a hug. I felt so relieved—not being mad at each other anymore was all I really wanted.

"Wait, how come we didn't hear about any of this?" Natalie asked.

"I wanted to do everything with just Ethan and me," I admitted. "I guess for Kindness Week, I wasn't very kind."

There was a split second of silence. Then Emily, Natalie, and Alana all broke out in huge smiles.

"Let's quit talking," Alana said. "We have a lot of decorating to do!" We all headed to the kitchen.

My heart lifted as I explained to the Mini Cupcake Club what Ethan and I had in mind. "But the problem is that we can't figure out a good way to fit the messages on the cupcakes," I said.

"I've got an idea," Emily said. She turned to Alana. "Do you have any toothpicks?"

Alana nodded and reached into a cabinet before handing a box of toothpicks to Emily.

Emily thought for a minute. "Let me try something," she said. She spread a thin, smooth layer of the chocolate frosting on a cupcake. Then she put it in the freezer just long enough for the frosting to get cold and harden. Next, she dipped a toothpick in the vanilla frosting and wrote out B KIND, one stroke at a time, one dip at a time. It took her under a minute and it worked perfectly!

"You're a genius!" I told Emily. We quickly frosted the cupcakes and put them in the freezer for five minutes. Then I took them out.

"Everyone, grab a toothpick. Or should I say, your writing wands!" Emily said.

We all started laughing.

"What's going on?" Alana's mom popped her head into the kitchen from the living room.

"Just having some maximum fun," Ethan said.

"Yeah. Maximum fun with the Mini Cupcake Club!" Alana added, and we all giggled again.

It felt so good to have my friends back!

Chapter 7

Special Delivery for a Special Friend

Using Emily's toothpick method, the five of us finished writing little messages on the kindness cupcakes in no time. Then it was a simple wrap with the cellophane, and the girls loved my ribbon idea. With every cupcake done, we were good to go. We even had two to spare! I gave them both to Alana.

"It's an apology for being unkind to you," I said.

Alana handed one back to me. "I accept your apology," she said. "And I would love to eat a cupcake with my friend."

I laughed as we pretended to clink our cupcakes together like glasses. Then we popped them in our mouths.

They were delicious.

"All right," I said after finishing my cupcake, "time to pack up our special deliveries!"

We divided the cupcakes into five containers holding thirteen mini cupcakes each, and each of us took one home. We agreed to meet one hour early at school the next morning. I couldn't wait for us to deliver our Kindness Week cupcakes!

Chapter 8

The Mini Cupcake Club of Kindness

We'd gotten Principal Estrella's permission to hand out our cupcakes before classes started. After everything that had happened, I felt exhausted, but also so glad that the rest of the club had swooped in to save the day. Without them, Ethan and I would have never gotten everything done in time.

All anyone in our grade could talk about for the rest of the day were our kindness cupcakes. Before the last bell rang, Principal Estrella even announced that she wanted to make them a yearly event!

I called a celebratory meeting at my house after school. When Ethan arrived, he was bouncing up and down. "Everyone loved our cupcakes!" he told us. "Every person I passed in the halls asked when we were going to make them again. Lots of students said they loved the encouraging things the cupcakes said, like 'Smile' and 'B Happy'!"

As we were hanging out in the living room, I gave Alana a big hug. "Thanks for being such a great friend," I told her.

"Anytime!" she replied.

I turned to the rest of the group. "And thank you, everyone, for pitching in to help. Ethan and I could never have done this without you." I told them to hold on a minute, and I ran into the kitchen. I returned with five cupcakes I'd decorated with the words U R THE BEST.

"I think this calls for a group kindness hug!" Natalie declared.

"Yes! Group kindness hug!" Emily repeated and opened her arms wide.

"And a cupcake!" I said, and everyone laughed. Project Kindness Cupcakes was a huge success—thanks to the Mini Cupcake Club!

Still Hungry?

Here's a bite of the fourth book in the Cupcake Diaries: The New Batch series, *Alana's Cupcake Garden.*

Old vs. New

I felt like a zombie stumbling onto the school bus when my tablet buzzed. My best friends from my old school, Ruby and Hannah, were texting.

Once I was settled in a seat, I read Ruby's text:

> Ruby: We miss you! When can we get together?